Paddy Stories

Dawn Haddon

Published in 2013 by FeedARead.com Publishing – Arts Council funded

First Edition

A CIP catalogue record for this title is available from the British Library.

Cover design and illustrations: Dawn Haddon

Dawn Haddon is originally from New Malden, Surrey, UK and has always enjoyed writing, and particularly enjoyed writing the Paddy Stories. It all started on a social network site in a virtual fairy garden. In the game Dawn would water gardens with her two westie girls Rosie and Lily. A couple of her visitors were Dionyssia and her westie Paddy, and Gilly with her westie Alfie. A few lines of comments became a regular adventure update. These lovely westies are now at Rainbow Bridge, and after chatting with Dionyssia and Gilly Dawn decided to write what she calls Paddy Stories in memory of them.

This lovely children's book with Sir Paddy, Sir Alfie, Lady Rosie, and Lady Lily has been a joy to write.

Connect with Dawn:

https://www.smashwords.com/profile/view/Sunrise2012
http://www.facebook.com/DawnsPaddyStories?ref=stream
uk.linkedin.com/pub/dawn-haddon/64/31a/287/
http://www.twitter.com/Sunrisefairy

Dedicated to the memory of our four special westies - Paddy, Alfie, Rosie and Lily

My thanks to Dionyssia Voridi (Sir Paddy) and Gilly Crane (Sir Alfie) for suggesting I put our adventures into print.

And thanks to my husband Brian for his help and hard work in finalising the cover design and illustrations.

Paddy Stories

Contents

Westie Kingdom

This is the story of wonderful westies who live far away in a magical kingdom full of beauty and happiness. Everything of beauty that you can imagine surrounding the westie kingdom is special, and one particular westie called Sir Paddy is the hero of our story.

Sir Paddy is a very handsome westie, bold and brave protector of all. He lives in a wonderful garden on the outskirts of Fairyland with a few silly chicks who act as his squires, snails, horses and a few other animals. Well, the trouble those chicks get themselves into sometimes

9

causes Sir Paddy a big headache! The silly chicks love to play tricks which ultimately go wrong, and sometimes make them look very silly indeed. There is one particular story which comes to mind, and it happened on a day when Sir Paddy was out patrolling the magical forests of Fairyland.

As Sir Paddy mounted his trusty steed 'Lancelot', a magnificent white horse with the longest mane of all the horses that lived in the garden, he had no idea of what the silly chicks were planning. He trotted off with his head held high and of course a tasty snack for later. As soon as he disappeared from sight the silly chicks all jumped into the air excited about their plan.

Chirpy the leader thought it would be a good idea to swap their straw bed for Sir Paddy's lovely soft mattress. The five of them rushed to Sir Paddy's bedroom only to find the door had been locked. It was then that one of the chicks noticed that the window was open, so they all rushed at the same time to get in. There were feathers everywhere and a lot of clucking, which of course aroused the snails. Danny, the head snail, came over to see what all the fuss was about and nearly fell over laughing to see the silly chicks in a big heap on the floor.

"What do you think you are doing you silly chicks?"

Chirpy was not amused and told Danny to mind his own business.

"Lucky for you Commando Kit is on training at the moment, you better clean all this mess up."

Commando Kit is a specialist elite snail who does a lot of intelligence work for Sir Paddy, and he was on a training day with the Special Forces snails. The silly chicks dusted themselves off and Chirpy jumped up and got in to Sir Paddy's bedroom. He lost no time in opening the door so the other silly chicks could rush in. Now, dragging the mattress off the bed was not too bad, but trying to get it through the door was another matter.

Meanwhile Sir Paddy was enjoying his ride through the forest. He was exploring a new path, and that's when he saw them. It was like a magical vision with two of the most beautiful lady westies he had ever seen. They were playing in their garden under the watchful eye of their fairy guardian. Sir Paddy was so focused on the beautiful westies playing he did not see the tree branch he was approaching. Before he knew it he was spinning round and round on this branch like a circus acrobat. He finally managed to gain control and stand up on the branch. Not wanting to look a fool in front of these two maidens he gave them a hearty wave, and the biggest westie smile he could muster. Then he heard the cracking of the branch and knew it was going to break and he would end up on his tail. Luckily at that moment the fairy guardian called to girls.

"Lady Rosie, Lady Lily, time for your nap my darlings."

Sir Paddy thought to himself 'Hmm, Lady R.......' it was at this point the branch broke and he started falling. The next thing he knew he was on Lancelot's back.

"Thank you Lancelot you saved me from a nasty fall."

"You're welcome Sir Paddy, but I will have to have a lay down when we get back and perhaps the silly chicks could give me a massage."

Sir Paddy wondered if he had gained a little weight, because why would Lancelot want a massage? Lancelot was a big horse and surely catching him would not be a problem. Sir Paddy was soon thinking of the girls again.

"Do you know who those westie girls are?"

"I have heard they are called Lady Rosie and Lady Lily, and live with their guardian fairy 'Sunrise'."

"I think we will send an invite to them to join us for tea one day, time for home now I think the kingdom is safe and well."

"Sunrise, Sunrise, who was that handsome westie boy?" cried Lady Rosie and Lady Lily excitedly together.

"That was Sir Paddy, Knight of the westie table and protector of all."

Before the girls could say another word Sunrise put her finger to her lips. "Shh my darlings, you will meet Sir Paddy very soon. Be patient."

Sunrise knew the branch that Sir Paddy was on was cracking, and had called the girls just before it broke. She also knew that Lancelot would catch him and all would be well.

As Sir Paddy entered his garden he could not believe the sight before his eyes. The mattress from his bed stuck in his bedroom doorway with two chicks stuck each side and one stuck at the top. The snails were all standing around laughing. Sir Paddy jumped off his horse.

"What an earth has been going on here?"

Danny the snail was only too happy to explain. "The the silly chicks wanted to change their straw bed for your nice soft mattress, they thought you wouldn't notice." Danny was now rolling about the floor laughing. "Well they got themselves stuck."

"Well I can't leave the place for 5 minutes and you lot are up to no good again."

Commando Kit had returned and was not impressed with what he saw.

"Leave this to me Sir Paddy, take my quarters and rest while I get the snails to release the silly chicks."

"Thank you Commando Kit, and join me for dinner when you are ready."

Commando Kit bowed to Sir Paddy then issued instructions for 'Operation Release'. He also told the silly chicks they would be on sweeping duty for 2 days.

Sunshine and Lollipops

It couldn't have been a better day for Lancelot. The sun was shining and he was enjoying a well earned back rub from the silly chicks. Well, after Sir Paddy had landed on his back when the tree branch broke Lancelot felt in the need for some pampering.

The silly chicks were not impressed, and Chirpy the head chick had a plan. He signalled for them to lean in nearer and whispered to the other chicks.

"Why don't we give the show-off Lancelot a shower?"

The chicks were all trying to stop laughing and they all nodded that it was a very good idea. So while two of the chicks carried on with the back rub, Chirpy and the two other chicks went to fetch some very cold water from the magical stream.

Sir Paddy was still thinking about Lady Rosie, and Lady Lily. How beautiful they were dressed in their pretty pink flowing gowns. He was also looking forward to the arrival of Sir Alfie, another westie knight in the neighbouring wood. Sir Paddy and Sir Alfie had been through westie knight training together and had a very strong bond.

The snails were busy preparing invitations for Lady Rosie, Lady Lily, and their guardian fairy Sunrise to come for a barbeque at the weekend. The invites had to be perfect as per Sir Paddy's orders, covered with flowers from the garden. Commando Kit was keeping a close eye on operations. He always kept his group of snail officers in check.

Lancelot had drifted off to sleep now and was completely unaware of the silly chick's plans. He was dreaming of his friend Alfonso, Sir Alfie's trusty steed a magnificent Palomino. They would share a nice glass of Pimm's later and some vol-au-vents, then perhaps a stroll to the nearby field to graze on the greenest grass of the kingdom. The day would be finished off with Lancelot's favourite lollipops and a nice cup of tea.

Commando Kit decided to take a stroll to the magical stream to do his usual security checks, and that's when he saw them. One of the silly chicks had got his claw caught on the bucket and was floating off down the steam. There was a lot of clucking and feathers flying with Chirpy and the other chick running round and round in circles before Chirpy grabbed the rope, and attempted to lasso the bucket. He ended up lassoing himself to the other chick. Commando Kit lost no time in untangling the silly chicks, then successfully lassoing the bucket and bringing the other silly chick safely back. They all knew they were in big trouble.

"You can explain exactly what was going on later. I have security checks to do. Now on the double straight back to base and report to my office 18:00 sharp."

Chirpy and the other two chicks rushed back to base only to find Lancelot asleep and snoring loudly with no sign of the other two chicks. Lancelot let out a great big raspberry, which made all the chicks jump. He was up on was his feet in no time thanking the chicks for a good back rub before trotting off. The silly chicks were confused but glad that he had not noticed the other chicks missing. They were in enough trouble already. It wasn't long before they discovered where the other two chicks had disappeared to, and this would be worse than explaining the water incident to Commando Kit.

A small trunk was beside a rock nearby and the sound of excited silly chicks could be heard inside. When Chirpy and the other chicks opened the lid there were the two other chicks tucking into Lancelot's lollipops. The chicks let out a huge gasp.
"What are you doing?" cried Chirpy.
The two chicks laughed and held up lollipops for the others to share. "Commando Kit caught us by the magical stream and he had to rescue Fluffy here." Fluffy was shaking his head and pointing to himself. "If he finds out about this we will be on extra duties for a month."
The two chicks threw the lollipops and jumped out of the trunk. Chirpy hid them under the other lollipops hoping Lancelot would not notice they had been nibbled. The silly chicks quickly ran off and hid in their chick house not daring to go out until the appointment with Commando Kit.

A little later Sir Paddy heard the arrival of his good friend Sir Alfie, and the two greeted each other with lots of tail wagging and excited barking. Alfonso had trotted off to meet Lancelot who had a glass of Pimm's waiting. The chicks were on their way to Commando Kit's office. Chirpy knocked on the door.
"Come in."
The silly chicks all rushed in at once and nearly fell over. Even the two that were not at the stream had come along, not wanting to be in the chick house alone in case Lancelot noticed the nibbled lollipops. Chirpy took a deep breath and stepped forward.

"Well sir we just thought it would a nice idea to bring some fresh cool water for Lancelot, just in case…….in case he wanted to dab his ears."

"Hmm, sounds a likely story to me, and I think you chicks were up to mischief again."

Before the chicks could answer Commando Kit silenced them with a wave of his hand.

"The barn needs cleaning out ready for the weekend, and I shall inspect it in two days, dismissed."

The chicks didn't argue. They knew they could not fool the Commando, he is just too clever. So with beaks down they made their way to the barn.

Everyone else was having a lovely time. Sir Paddy and Sir Alfie were chatting about old times, and of course the discovery of Lady Rosie and Lady Lily. Lancelot and Alfonso had been to the field and were now enjoying a lollipop each with a nice cup of tea, fortunately not noticing the nibbled ones. The snails were having a nice glass of lemonade and biscuits with Commando Kit, and the silly chicks were working their feathers off in the barn. It had been an eventful day full of sunshine and lollipops.

Magical Barbeque

There was great excitement in the Sparkle Garden. Lady Rosie and Lady Lily were looking forward to their shopping trip with Sunrise. They will pick out a special outfit each for the barbeque this afternoon at Sir Paddy's garden. Sunrise had another surprise for them too.

"Girls, Sir Paddy is sending a limousine to collect us all, he has also sent you both a satin cape to wear - red for Lady Rosie, and pink for

Lady Lily. Now girls we must go and get you a special dress each, and perhaps a small gift for Sir Paddy."

"Oh Sunrise, can I get Sir Paddy a silk scarf?" asked Lady Rosie.

"And can I get Sir Paddy a silk bow-tie?" asked Lady Lily.

"We shall get Sir Paddy the finest silk scarf and bow-tie we can find. Now girls you need to have your nails done as well so we better get a wriggle on."

Lady Rosie and Lady Lily loved it when Sunrise said 'wriggle on', it always made them laugh, and they went off wriggling their tails.

Commando Kit went to inspect the barn for the barbeque later. He had sent the snails in to help the silly chicks, because it had to look perfect.

"Good job men, Sir Paddy will be very happy when he sees this."

The snails all bowed and smiled at each other. The silly chicks stood there nervously waiting for Commando Kit to speak to them.

"You have worked hard chicks."

At this point all the chicks fell in a big lump on the barn floor very relieved that the Commando seemed pleased.

"You may go and join the snails for a well earned cup of tea and some angel cake."

Before Commando Kit could say another word the silly chicks had disappeared from the barn, just a few feathers were left on the spot they were all huddled. He did have a smile on his face although he would not let the chicks know it had amused him.

Sir Paddy had spent the morning at the gym; well he wanted to look his best. He was in his bedroom and could not decide what to wear. Should he put on the blue shirt or the yellow one? While he was looking in the mirror Sammy, the beautiful yellow and lilac butterfly, flew in the window and landed on his shoulder.

"Hello Sir Paddy. I think the yellow shirt; you will look very handsome in it." Sir Paddy was blushing but was very happy for the advice.

"Thank you Sammy butterfly, I want to look my best for Lady Rosie and Lady Lily and of course their fairy guardian Sunrise."

Sammy butterfly circled round Sir Paddy twice then flew back out the window again. She knew her job was done.

Danny the head snail was making sure everything was ready for later on. There were lovely red lanterns hung all round the barn, and flowers on the tables. The snails would also be playing the music tonight, and they had set up their instruments in a corner of the barn. Outside Commando Kit was supervising the barbeque that Lancelot was preparing. He was also making sure the silly chicks stayed well away from the barbeque so he had them putting balloons and rose petals all along the driveway. Of course you would hear the occasional bang when one of the balloons burst, usually because one of the silly chicks had either blown it up too much or sat on it when they got tired! Well at least he knew where they were and what they were up too.

It was nearly time for the limousine to arrive. The girls looked beautiful in their lacy gowns. Lady Rosie's was cream with little red butterflies and the red cape Sir Paddy had sent went perfect with her gown. Lady Lily's was lilac with pink butterflies, which matched her pink cape too. A big white limo was now pulling up and out jumped a very smartly dressed white bunny who was the chauffer.

"Good afternoon Lady Rosie, Lady Lily, and Sunrise. Please step into the limo, there are some refreshment inside waiting for you."

The girls and Sunrise jumped inside and were amazed at how wonderful it was. There were disco lights and very comfy seats. Lemonade drinks with a few nibbles to keep them going until they got to Sir Paddy's. Sunrise smiled when she saw how happy and excited the girls were, and she knew it was going to be a perfect afternoon.

Sammy the butterfly landed on Commando Kit's shoulder.

"The limousine is approaching Commando Kit."

"Thank you Sammy you are most welcome to stay and enjoy the barbeque."

Sammy flew round Commando Kit and told him she would love to stay. Danny the head snail had seen the limo approaching too. He signalled to the silly chicks to stand either side of the drive and wave flags as the limo passed by. Soon the limo pulled up and the bunny jumped out to open the doors for the girls. When they stepped out of the limo the chicks beaks just dropped to the floor because they looked so beautiful. Fluffy stumbled back and fell onto one of the balloons which went off bang. The girls screamed with surprise, and Sir Paddy looked very cross. After a moment of silence Sunrise gave the Lady Rosie and Lady Lily a big hug then they all laughed out loud.

"It's ok Sir Paddy no harm done, and your garden looks magnificent. Everyone has done a wonderful job."

Sunrise turned to Commando Kit and Danny and bowed her head. Everyone was smiling, the food was now cooking, and the music was playing. The girls gave their gifts to Sir Paddy and he immediately put on the silk scarf and bow tie.

Yes this was a magical barbeque, everyone was happy and the evening flowers gave off a lovely scent. It was quite late when the limo took Sunrise and the girls back home, and that night Sir Paddy dreamt of the beautiful Lady Rosie and Lady Lily.

Fanfare and Fireworks

♪♪Da da da ♫ Tra la♪ 'What a perfect day,' thought Danny the head snail, as the trumpet's melody harmonised in the dancing gentle breeze. The sky was deep blue with not a cloud to be seen. The sun was smiling down its warm rays, and there was happiness throughout the garden. Today was a special day, because Commando Kit will be receiving the highest honour medal for his bravery and courage serving Sir Paddy in the magical kingdom.

A few months ago there was a rumour about a fire breathing dragon who wanted to rule the magical kingdom. Sir Paddy and Commando Kit with a couple of his officer snails had set off to find the dragon, and to escort him out of the magical forests of Fairyland. It didn't take long for them to find him, and he was a very big dragon sleeping by a large rock. Sir Paddy wanted to confront him immediately, but Commando Kit advised against this until he was sure Sir Paddy was in no danger.

"My men will surround the dragon Sir Paddy." Commando Kit was speaking in low tones so the dragon would not hear them and wake up. "I am going to wrap some of these tree vines," he pointed to the floor, "around his mouth, because when he wakes the first thing he will probably do is breathe fire."

Before Sir Paddy could say another word the two snails were in place and Commando Kit was wrapping the vines around the dragon's mouth. It was at this point that they all turned round to see an even bigger dragon, and very cross with its arms crossed ready to breathe fire on them all. Commando Kit lost no time shouting "take cover" to his men, and grabbing Sir Paddy, so he was clear out of the line of fire. The dragon breathed its firey breath just enough to scorch the vines so the other dragon was free. Commando Kit went to face the dragon immediately, he had realised that this was a mother protecting her baby.

"Commando Kit ma'am."

He bowed to her. Sir Paddy and the two snails were amazed.

"Apologies for the vines but I had to protect my men and Sir Paddy from any risk of fire breathing."

The large dragon nodded her head while the smaller one ran behind her.

"I have heard of your bravery Commando Kit, and wish no harm to you, Sir Paddy or your men. My son and I are travelling to the magical caves beyond the magical forests, but some naughty magpies stole our golden coins so we were unable to make a wish to fly."

"Allow me." Sir Paddy gave the dragon a small bag of gold coins.

"We had been informed that a fire breathing dragon wanted to rule the magical kingdom, I see now that perhaps those naughty magpies had been spreading rumours. Please accept our apologies."

Sir Paddy bowed his head and the dragon did the same. Commando Kit eventually found the naughty magpies, retrieved the gold, and sent them on a course to learn flower arranging.

Sir Paddy was happy that morning singing in the shower thinking about the day ahead. He was looking forward to presenting the medal to his brave and trusted friend Commando Kit, and to the arrival of his most favourite girls in the world, Lady Rosie and Lady Lily, who will be escorted by his good friend Sir Alfie. He could hear the trumpets in the distance, and the smell of lavender floating in the air. Sir Paddy bushed his teeth, combed his hair, and put on some on his 'West Spice' splash. Now he was ready to put on his blue dress uniform with the white peak cap, and white gloves.

Lady Rosie and Lady Lily were very excited running about and barking with joy. They each had a new dress and hat to wear. Lady Rosie's dress was white with red roses, and a red hat. Lady Lily's was white with pink roses, and a pink hat.

"Girls it is time for you to put your new dresses on - Sir Alfie will be here shortly to escort us to Sir Paddy's garden, and there is another surprise for you both."

Both the girls gasped and put their paws to their mouths waiting for Sunrise to speak.

"Sir Paddy has arranged for the rainbow crown carriage to collect us," Sunrise paused for a moment while she observed the sparking joy in her girl's eyes. "And......the magical unicorn Greg will guide the carriage for us."

Lady Rosie and Lady Lily were so excited they both ran round in circles chasing their tails and barking.

The silly chicks were bored. Everything was ready for the medal ceremony at 11am. They had put out all the flags along the driveway, and got the tables ready for the jacket potatoes that were cooking for later that day. Chirpy the leader was cross and complained to the other chicks. "That head snail Danny is bossy."

The other chicks all nodded in agreement.

"We only wanted to help with the firework display. He was very rude saying we were not allowed to help because it was a dangerous job and we were too silly."

"Very rude, very rude," The other chicks all cried out together.

Chirpy stamped his foot but did not see the rock and stubbed his toe.

"Ow, ow." Chirpy danced around holding his foot.

"There are some sparklers left why don't we put them on the tables, and when everyone comes for the potatoes we can light them? We will start the firework display early."

Beaky was very pleased with himself and waited for Chirpy to agree.

"Yes there are Beaky, they are all busy getting dressed. Sparks you sneak under the shed and get the sparklers. Meet us at the tables."

Sparks nodded and rushed off.

"Cluck, go and look for some matches."

Ten minutes later they were all back at the tables.

"This is a big sparkler Sparks and you only have two of them. Well we better test one now."

There was great excitement, and Chirpy wedged the sparkler into the middle of the table through a crack in the wood. Cluck gave the matches to Chirpy. He struck the match and was just about to light the sparkler when he heard a familiar voice.

"Blow that match out immediately!"

They all froze, and turned round slowly to see Commando Kit standing in his full dress uniform looking very splendid indeed. He was not smiling, and the silly chicks knew they were in trouble. Chirpy blew out the match and dropped it to the floor. Commando Kit marched up to them.

"What are you doing with the two display rockets? ....And why were you trying to light them and put yourself and everyone else in danger?"

"We....we just wanted to make the tables look nice with the sparklers sir."

Commando Kit realised the mistake the silly chicks had made, and thankfully he had stopped them lighting the rocket in time.

"Come with me."

Commando Kit took the rockets and the matches from the chicks and marched off. The silly chicks followed nervously, and soon they

24

arrived at the firework shed. Commando Kit put the rockets safely away and produced a sparkler for each of the silly chicks.

"Come to me after the medal parade and I will light the sparklers for you. Do not go near the shed again. Is that clear?"

The silly chicks all nodded together, and were in awe of Commando Kit's kindness to them. Commando Kit was wise and knew the silly chicks would behave now, which meant he could go have and a glass of wine with Sir Paddy before Lady Rosie and Lady Lily arrived.

The rainbow crown carriage pulled by the magical unicorn Greg arrived, shortly followed by Sir Alfie on his trusty seed Alfonso. Sir Alfie jumped down from Alfonso and bowed low to Lady Rosie and Lady Lily. He then turned and bowed low to Sunrise.

"Welcome Sir Alfie, there are some chilled drinks of lemonade ready for you, Alfonso, and Greg. You must all be a little parched on this beautiful sunny day."

"Thank you Sunrise - that would be most acceptable. If you and the ladies would like to make yourselves comfortable in the carriage we will be leaving in 5 minutes."

Sunrise nodded in acknowledgement. Lady Rosie and Lady Lily giggled as they skipped to the carriage. They thought Sir Alfie looked very handsome in his uniform.

The medal ceremony went smoothly, and Sir Paddy had a tear in his eye when he pinned the medal on Commando Kit. The potatoes were cooked perfectly, and everyone enjoyed them. The firework display was spectacular. The silly chicks went to Commando Kit after the parade for him to light their sparklers. They were having such fun until Beaky spun round and round in circles, and got so dizzy he fell over and scorched Fluffy's tail feathers. Luckily Danny the snail was near by keeping an eye on them via Commando Kit's orders. He immediately threw a bucket of cold water over Fluffy then rolled all over the floor laughing at him. Danny knew he only needed to throw a little water over the chick, but thought they could do with being taught a lesson. As he was getting up from the floor he noticed Commando Kit looking at him with one eyebrow raise, and knew he disapproved of his actions. Danny rushed and got a towel to dry Fluffy who was not very pleased with him, and spat a load of water and feathers in

Danny's face. Commando Kit turned away as he did not want them to see the amusement on his face after a day of fanfare and fireworks.

Glittering Grand Ball

After the wonderful medal ceremony in honour of Commando Kit for his courage and bravery, a glittering Ball was to be held the very next day. This caused great excitement throughout the magical kingdom, where joy and laughter could be heard.

In the Sparkle Garden on the day of the Ball Lady Rosie and Lady Lily had spent the morning at the Spa for beauty treatments, and then went on to have their hair and nails done. It was time for them to put on their ball gowns. Lady Rosie wore a gold silk gown covered with sequins in black and gold swirl patterns. Lady Lily wore a silver silk gown also covered in sequins in opaque and silver diamond patterns. They both had diamante Alice bands to wear. Sir Paddy had sent them a corsage each to wear on their paws. Sunrise stood back with her hands together smiling. "How beautiful my girls look tonight."

Lady Rosie and Lady Lily ran to Sunrise and they all hugged each other.

Sir Alfie had stayed at Sir Paddy's after the ceremony, and it was while they were getting ready for the Ball that day that all the commotion occurred. Bang, Crash, Bang! Sir Paddy and Sir Alfie stopped adjusting their bow ties, and looked at each other for a moment then ran outside to see what all the noise was about. There was no surprise to discover the silly chicks were involved, and there they all were in a big heap, feathers flying on the floor with what looked like part of the chick house roof.

"What has happened here?" Cried Danny the head snail as he came running over. Danny could not believe what he was seeing, there was no doubt it was part of the chick house roof. "What is part of the chick house roof doing here?"

The chicks had picked themselves up by now, and they were all looking at the ground too scared to speak. Danny was about to speak again when Sir Paddy silenced him by raising his paw.

"Now young chicks would you like to explain to me what has happened, or would you like me to call Commando Kit back from his well-earned leave so you can explain to him, hmm?"

Chirpy the leader stepped forward to speak to Sir Paddy. "Well Sir Paddy we were sliding down the roof just where the water leaks onto it from the gutter….and, and we thought we would all slide down as a train a......"

"And that's when it happened," cried Fluffy. "The roof wobbled a little bit and then we took off and it was so much fun……..and then….."

"And then we started to drop and ended up here," piped up Sparks.

"Don't worry Sir Paddy we will soon get this mess sorted out," explained Danny, as he walked over to Sir Paddy and Sir Alfie. "A good friend of mine Andy Bear…" Everyone gasped at the mention of a bear except the silly chicks who had tried to lift a piece of roof, which they were now stuck under. "No, no it's ok. Andy is a magical friendly bear, and he has helped out before. Andy Bear has great respect for Sir Paddy and Commando Kit. The fairies have put a magical spell on him to help protect the magical forests and all who live here."

Sir Paddy nodded his head and requested Andy Bear be brought to him for introduction before he left for the Ball.

Andy Bear had heard all the noise in Sir Paddy's garden and was wondering what had happened. Sammy the beautiful butterfly appeared and landed on a lavender bush.

"Hello Andy Bear the silly chicks have managed to bring off and lose a section of the roof for the chick house. Sir Paddy and Sir Alfie are escorting Lady Rosie and Lady Lily to the glittering Grand Ball this evening. Your help is required in the garden to clear the mess, and mend the chick house roof."

"No problem Sammy, I am on my way. Does Sir Paddy know that I will help? I don't want to alarm anyone."

"Danny has told Sir Paddy and it is ok. Sir Paddy would like to meet you before he leaves for the ball this evening."

"I will introduce myself to Sir Paddy first."

Andy Bear jumped to his feet to make his way to the garden; he was only 5 minutes away. Sammy circled Andy Bear twice and then landed on his head to stay with him until he had spoken with Sir Paddy.

Commando Kit was due back the next day, and the silly chicks were worried about what he would say when he hears about the roof. They had managed to free themselves from the piece of roof.

"We are going to be on sweeping duty for a week," cried Fluffy

"Maybe two!" added Cluck

"Or..." Beaky's eyes were wide and he looked scared. "He will make us go on a training trip with him, and walk ten miles."

All the silly chicks gasped together. At this point they were all running around in circles panicking with Spark shouting, "Don't panic!"

"Stop!" was bellowing out to the silly chicks, and when they saw it was Andy Bear they all froze on the spot. Danny rushed over to greet him shaking his big paw, and the chick's beaks fell open. Sammy the butterfly went over to the silly chicks and told them not to be afraid.

Danny lost no time in introducing Andy Bear to Sir Paddy and Sir Alfie, and after a quick chat with Sammy as well all was well in the garden. In no time Andy Bear got to work moving the roof back, and with the help of the snails the roof was securely fixed in place.

Lady Rosie and Lady Lily could hear the roar of the engine as the elegant red sports car with the roof down approached. Sir Paddy and Sir Alfie jumped out, and they both looked so handsome in the dinner suits and black bow ties. They helped the girls into the car, and Sunrise was waving them off just as the sun was starting to set. The girl's dresses sparkled in the dimming glow of the sunlight.

When they reached the red carpet entrance to the ball Commando Kit had arrived, and would join them for dinner. The door was opened for them and the band was playing a wonderful Glen Miller tune. They all entered the glittering Grand Ball together.

Spellbound Evening

"I could have danced all night, I could have danced all night, and stilllllll have danced some more." Sir Paddy was singing at the top of his voice dancing round the study while his good friend Sir Alfie was listening. He was so happy after spending the night at the grand glittering ball with his two most favourite girls in the world, Lady Rosie and Lady Lily, and his best friend and fellow knight Sir Alfie, and not forgetting the brave Commando Kit who had joined them for

dinner that evening. Sir Paddy wanted to share a mug of hot chocolate with Sir Alfie who would be leaving in the morning to go back to the neighbouring kingdom.

"It was a splendid evening and the girls looked beautiful," said Sir Alfie, who then lifted his hot chocolate mug up and made a toast.

"To Lady Rosie, Lady Lily, and to the brave Commando Kit. To a spellbound evening!" Sir Paddy immediately lifted his hot chocolate mug to click Sir Alfie's, and together they toasted to the evening.

"Spellbound evening."

Sunrise was looking at Lady Rosie's and Lady Lily's ball gowns that were now safely hanging up in their wardrobes. 'How beautiful my girls looked tonight, and how handsome Sir Paddy and Sir Alfie had looked in their black tie and dinner suits,' thought Sunrise to herself. She started humming the tune, 'There must be magic in the air' (the version sung by Johnny Matthus) because everywhere she looked there was coloured stardust. Lady Rosie and Lady Lily were fast asleep. The little darlings had danced so much that as soon as they got into bed they went straight to sleep. Sunrise didn't even have time to make them hot chocolate that evening for their bed time chat before lights out.

The silly chicks had stayed in the chick house all evening after the roof fiasco. They were all very bored by now, and Chirpy had decided to sneak out to see if the lovely red sports car that Sir Paddy and Sir Alfie used was back. If it was then he would know that everyone would be in bed so they could then sneak off to the kitchen.

"Sssschhhhh," said Chirpy to the others. "I will give you two clucks if it is all clear, then everyone can come out and follow me."

There was lots of wing flapping and excitement, and they all started to get a bit noisy.

"Sssschhhhh, I have to make sure they are all in bed," whispered Chirpy. Silently he crept out from the chick house taking very big exaggerated steps, while the other 4 chicks, who were virtually on top of each other, peered round the door.

It was all going so well until Fluffy, who was on the top, started to wobble. Chirpy was almost at the gate and he could see the red sports car. As he turned to signal to the others he saw Fluffy falling. Running to catch him he tripped on a bucket and got his foot caught. Chirpy went into a ball and headed straight for the other chicks like a ball at the ten pin bowling. Before Fluffy had hit the ground Chirpy had bowled into them all, and it was a full on strike. What a noise this created and the feathers were flying. As they all lay on the floor rubbing their beaks and bottoms a very large shadow covered them all. Jumping up together and clucking in confusion then running into each other they heard a very powerful and strong "Stop!"

It was Andy the magical bear. He had decided to keep an eye on the silly chicks while Sir Paddy and Sir Alfie were at the grand glittering ball. Andy had just dozed for a moment when he had heard some noises, and realised the silly chicks were up to no good again.

"If Sir Paddy or Sir Alfie has been disturbed Commando Kit will hear about this."

There was a big gasp from all the silly chicks together.

"Now not another word and straight to bed, and remember I am just outside." All the chicks nodded and rushed straight to bed. Not another word was heard from them all evening. Luckily Sir Paddy and Sir Alfie had not been disturbed and their lights were still off. Andy Bear did not move from the chick house gate all night. He had decided as no harm was done and no one was disturbed he would not bother Commando Kit in the morning. Andy was remembering the scrapes he had got himself into as a young cub. He felt very happy, and was glad he had been able to be of service for Sir Paddy, albeit that Sir Paddy and Commando Kit would probably never know.

Unbeknown to Andy Bear Greg the magical unicorn had observed all. He had been visiting Lancelot and Alfico, who were Sir Paddy's and Sir Alfie's trusted steeds. Greg had just wondered back from the magical stream after a refreshing drink, and stretching his legs and magical wings. He saw Andy Bear's kindness, and how well he had handled the silly chicks. Indeed he would let Sir Paddy know what a good job he had done in the morning. Greg had circled the chick house with a spell to keep the noise from waking everyone up.

All was quiet in the Sparkle Garden while Lady Rosie and Lady Lily were dreaming about the wonderful spellbound evening.....

How grand it was with the band playing, and the glittering lights all over the ceiling like shining stars. What a splendid meal with excellent food served, and how handsome Sir Paddy and Sir Alfie looked in their dinner suits and black bow ties. Commando Kit looked splendid in his full dress uniform wearing the medal Sir Paddy had presented to him. And as the girls danced the evening away with the boys all the lady snails were gathering around Commando Kit. Their shells were colourful and decorated with beautiful jewels that sparkled under the lights. One snail in particular, who had a larger shell than all the others, kept her dance card reserved only for Commando Kit. The girls found out she was called Dame Totty, and she ran a successful healthy eating pizza chain. Dame Totty had seen the girls with Sir Paddy and Sir Alfie talking to Commando Kit, and had wasted no time in joining them for a chat. How she loved chatting about the superior quality of the pizzas, and how she tries every one before they leave the fantasy range oven in Shady Leaf Meadow. Commando Kit raised one eyebrow at the thought of trying every pizza, because he had a very strict eating and exercise regime. He was far too polite to disagree with Dame Totty, and just smiled with the occasional nod. Commando Kit then whizzed Dame Totty round the dance floor, which was the most exercise she had done for ages. When the dance had finished she excused herself to powder her nose, and went off for a short nap. Lady Rosie and Lady Lily giggled to themselves because they had seen where Dame Totty had gone to for a sleep. Sir Paddy and Sir Alfie were aware that their good friend Commando Kit was in popular demand, and asked him if he would like to join them and the girls for a glass of champagne and some fresh air on the grand balcony. Sunrise smiled as the coloured stardust twinkled in the moon light, and the perfume of lotus blossoms filled the air of the spellbound evening.

Sparkling Reunion

Sunrise was excited because her good friend and guardian angel Eos would be visiting later that day. They had not seen each other for a whole twinkle year, because Eos had been busy spreading much joy and laughter throughout the Magical Kingdom.

Sir Paddy was excited too. He was very much looking forward to travelling to the Sparkle Garden later to see his most favourite girls in the world, Lady Rosie, and Lady Lily. There was another special person who he had not seen for some time, and he smiled as he remembered his guardian angel Eos who was his guardian while he was training at Knight School. Sir Paddy had spent all week at the gym because he wanted to look his best. As he stood in front of the full length mirror his left eyebrow rose up, and he smiled thinking he looked a very shapely westie indeed!

Everyone was excited, and even the silly chicks had been invited to the Sparkle Garden today. They were rushing around the chick house clucking away brushing down their feathers, and all gasped when they saw Chirpy. He had all his feathers on his head sticking up like a cockerel. Fluffy started to point and laugh, and within seconds the silly chicks were flapping about laughing. This quickly aroused the attention of Danny the head snail who went to see what all the noise was about.

The maypole looked splendid in the Sparkle Garden. The fluffy bunnies had been working very hard to get it ready in time so Lady Rosie, and Lady Lily could perform the Spring May dance for their very special visitor guardian angel Eos. The girls had beautiful white dresses with pink and yellow flowers, and Sunrise had put flowers in their hair. The maypole was very tall with 6 coloured ribbons attached. There was red, orange, yellow, green, blue, indigo and the maypole was violet - all the colours from the rainbow. The bunnies would be joining the girls in the May dance. The four bunnies had lemon dresses with little bows on. The Sparkle Garden looked so wonderful with coloured lanterns hanging, and pretty streamers attached to the chairs gently blowing in the breeze. A rainbow appeared over the garden, and Sunrise heard the sound of the carriage approaching she knew her good friend would be there any minute.

Sir Paddy and Commando Kit had heard the commotion too, and had gone outside to investigate.

"I suspect the noise is coming from the chick house Sir Paddy."

"Commando Kit." Sir Paddy acknowledged his friend with a nod. They both went straight to the chick house and saw Danny the head snail and the rest of the chicks in fits of laughter pointing at Chirpy. Both Sir Paddy and Commando Kit found their lips twitching into a smile, but both of them composed themselves immediately. Danny looked round and when he saw Sir Paddy and Command Kit standing there he immediately instructed the other chicks to be quiet.

"Sir!" He addressed both Sir Paddy and Commando Kit. "I'm afraid Chirpy had umm well.... made us all laugh."

"The coach has arrived to take everyone to the Sparkle Garden. Get the chicks and your men on board Danny. Sir Paddy and I will join you all shortly."

Danny nodded and the chicks all lined up behind him. Chirpy stood at the back of the queue and did not look at the other chicks because he was sulking. Everyone was quiet now, but both Sir Paddy and Commando Kit noticed that Danny and the other chicks were secretly still giggling, because they all had their heads down and their bodies were shaking.

Beautiful music played in the Sparkle Garden as the splendid carriage pulled up. It was white and trimmed with gold that sparkled in the sunlight. The golden unicorn called Brian had brought the carriage safely to a stop. Brian had completed his safety carriage driving course and gained gold standard. He was a member of 'MOSPA', the Magical Official Society for the Prevention of Accidents. The carriage door opened and Eos got out of the carriage. Sunrise immediately ran over to her dear friend closely followed by Lady Rosie, and Lady Lily.

"Dear Eos it has been far too long, I have missed you my good friend."

There was a tear in Sunrise's eye because her heart was so full of love.

"It is good to be back Sunrise, and look at the girls how pretty they look."

They all had a group hug with excessive tail wagging and barking from the girls.

"Let's go and have some tea because it won't be long until Sir Paddy, Commando Kit, and everyone arrives."

Sunrise pointed to a gazebo that had refreshments ready.

Everyone was singing on the coach 'The wheels of the bus go round and round.' Commando Kit was driving because he had his PSV licence, and he smiled at the rather out of tune singing. He could see the gates to the Sparkle Garden, and he could see the white and gold carriage which he knew belonged to Eos. How he was looking forward to seeing her again

The coach stopped, and as Commando Kit released the air brakes a loud whoosh noise made the silly chicks jump. Chirpy jumped so high he hit his head on the coach roof, and the cockerel style feathers immediately fell flat. Everyone was looking at him, and they all started laughing. Eos was now standing by the coach smiling at Chirpy, and when he saw her magical smile he started laughing too. It was a perfect afternoon with everyone chatting and happy. The unicorns Greg and Brian snacked on the magical oats Eos had brought for them. Andy Bear and Sammy the beautiful butterfly chatted with the bunnies about the maypole. Danny, Lancelot and the snails were waiting for Sir Alfie and his steed Alfonso, who would be arriving very soon. Lady Rosie and Lady Lily had gone off to get prepared for the maypole dance, leaving Eos, Sunrise, Sir Paddy and Commando Kit chatting.

"Oh Kitty Coos and 'ickle Paddy – I am so proud of my special boys." Eos gave them both a big hug and a kiss on each cheek. Both Commando Kit and Sir Paddy were blushing, and so happy to see Eos again. Eos had also mentored Commando Kit when he was at Commando training base. Sir Alfie had now arrived so the celebrations could begin.

The silly chicks were in big trouble again. They had decided to explore the Sparkle Garden when they came across the maypole.

"Wow look at that!" cried Beaky.

"Look at the pretty ribbons – I want to dance round the pole," said Cluck who then grabbed the red ribbon and started skipping round the pole. It was not long before all the chicks joined in, and were soon tangled up with each other. There was a gasp because Lady Rosie and Lady Lily had just arrived to get ready for the maypole dance.

"You silly chicks – look what you have done. The ribbons are all tangled now," cried Lady Rosie crossly.

"I don't think we can un-tangle them," cried Lady Lily. "What are we going to do Rosie?" As the girls stood there looking at the chaos caused by the silly chicks, Andy Bear and the bunnies arrived.

"Keep still chicks the bunnies will get you out, but we have to work quickly. Lady Rosie and Lady Lily can you go and stall everyone for 5 minutes?" The girls nodded and thanked Andy Bear for helping. They skipped off to delay everyone arriving at the maypole.

It was tricky, but the bunnies managed to release the silly chicks one by one. As they were trying to release the very last silly chick, Cluck, who was wriggling around a lot more than the other silly chicks, they noticed the red ribbon was wound round his beak. Cluck wriggled more and more until the ribbon had started shredding with the end piece falling to the ground. This was followed by a loud thud as Cluck landed on his beak. The bunnies, the other silly chicks who were sitting on the grass, and Andy Bear all gasped then giggled at the site of the silly chick with his beak stuck in the grass and his bottom sticking up. He was now free and he started coughing, spluttering and spitting bits of red ribbon out. He had been so tangled up there were still bits of red ribbon in his feathers. Andy Bear picked up the end piece of red ribbon from the ground, and was wondering how to fix it when lots of coloured sparkling stars appeared. He dropped the ribbons and when he looked again the maypole it was perfect again with no broken ribbons. The magical unicorns Greg and Brian had seen what had happened, and cast a spell to help Andy Bear.

The rest of the afternoon went without a hitch. The girls had sung, 'The Sun Has Got its Hat On,' before everyone went to watch the maypole dance. Most of the guests were unaware of what the silly chicks had done, although it was noticed that bits of red ribbon were in one of the silly chick's feathers. It was indeed a wonderful sparkling reunion.

Sunset Home Coming

Eos and Sunrise were having an early morning chat and cuppa before Lady Rosie and Lady Lily woke up.

"It is wonderful to be back Sunrise, and what a lovely afternoon yesterday."

Eos giggled, "Those silly chicks." She was laughing so much now she put on hands over her mouth. "The unicorns told me how they had got tangled in the maypole ribbons, and how Andy Bear had come to the rescue."

"Hmm, I am not surprised. Those silly chicks are always up to some sort of mischief, and I did notice bits of red ribbon on one of the silly chicks. Sir Paddy and Commando Kit always try and keep an eye on them."

They were both laughing now, and Sunrise was so happy her good friend was there. Eos took a sip of her tea then leaned forward in her chair to speak.

"Sunrise, I have some news."

Sunrise put down her cup wondering what her friend was going to tell her.

"I think my 'ickle Paddy and Kitty Coos could do with a bit of help with those silly chicks. It is time Paddy's garden had a guardian angel living there again."

"Eos that is wonderful news and I couldn't agree more. Sir Paddy and Commando Kit will be thrilled."

"I have arranged to meet them both for lunch tomorrow, and I will tell them then."

Just as Sunrise was going to reply, Lady Rosie and Lady Lily appeared. They had just woken up, and both rushed over to Eos to hug her with wagging tails.

Sir Paddy had arranged for a huge picnic to be set up down by the magical stream for lunch the next day. A marquee had been erected with a golden carpet inside, and a red carpet outside the entrance door. There were fairy lights inside the marquee, and the main table was decorated with butterfly shaped lanterns that would be lit with lavender smelling tea light. Sir Paddy knew Eos loved the smell of lavender, and he had also picked lavender as the theme colour.

"Sir Paddy everything is ready for tomorrow, and the bees have made some extra special honey to go on the pancakes," cried Danny the head snail.

Sir Paddy had just finished his mid-morning jog and was ready to take a shower.

"Good. Danny I will meet you down by the magical stream in half an hour. I want everything to be perfect for tomorrow – so make sure the silly chicks are behaving."

41

Danny saluted to Sir Paddy before going in the direction of the silly chick house. He knew the silly chicks were always up to something, and he was hoping they would all still be tucked up in their beds having a lay-in, and out of trouble.

Commando Kit stood by the magical stream and was very pleased with the good job Danny, the head snail, and his men had done with the marquee. There was no sign of the silly chicks so Commando Kit decided to go and have a shower. He had already completed a 20 mile run early that morning, and another 5 mile jog with Sir Paddy.

"He's gone, he's gone," cried Chirpy excitedly, and all the silly chicks jumped up and down and flapped their wings.

"Let's go inside," said Sparks pointing at the marquee…. "This is the biggest tent I've ever seen."

All the silly chicks agreed. None of them were supposed to be there. Normally they would not be up, unless they were in trouble and Commando Kit had assigned them to do punishment duty. Even after the maypole fiasco yesterday it seemed they had got away with that one. Cluck was still complaining that his beak hurt much to the amusement of the other silly chicks. The only reason they were at the magical stream was because of the smell….yes the smell of toasted marsh mallows. After the marquee had been erected Andy Bear and the snails were ready for a snack. Danny agreed to make everyone toasted marsh mallow, and that's why the silly chicks were hiding down at the magical stream. They had not expected Commando Kit to arrive after the snails and Andy Bear had left, they had also not expected to see such a large tent. The silly chicks being the silly chicks were now determined to explore inside the marquee, and Sparks was now rushing to the red carpet entrance closely followed by Chirpy, Beaky, Cluck and Fluffy.

Sir Paddy was just having a coffee on his terrace, and was looking forward to meeting Danny at the magical stream to see the marquee. Everything had to be perfect for Eos' visit tomorrow, and he knew there was something she wanted to tell him and Commando Kit.

'I hope she can stay for a while,' Paddy thought to himself. 'This garden needs a guardian angel – a woman's touch.' He sighed. What a beautiful day, the sun was shining and not a cloud in the sky except
………..

'What an earth is that,' said Sir Paddy to himself. At that moment Commando Kit arrived.

"Sir Paddy." Commando Kit's face had a look of disbelief on it. "We have a big problem and need to go to the magical stream now. I will explain en-route."

Sir Paddy jumped to his feet nearly knocking his chair over then they both made off at speed for the magical stream. There was no need for Commando Kit to explain because Sir Paddy could see exactly what the problem was.

"I don't believe this, how did it happen?" gasped Sir Paddy. Commando Kit was just about to answer when they arrived and saw the full scale of the situation. The marquee was floating at least 10 foot off the ground, but luckily the securing pegs were still in place. The silly chicks were screaming and clinging onto the red carpet, which was hanging down outside the marquee.

"It appears a bottle of helium gas, which had been turned on, was left in the marquee. Danny the head snail wanted to fill balloons that said 'Welcome' for Eos. Unfortunately he had not run this by me first because he wanted to surprise you sir."

"It was a nice idea of Danny's Commando Kit, but what are we going to do about rescuing the silly chicks?"

Sir Paddy raised his paws in the air. At that moment Andy Bear arrived with the magical unicorn Greg. Andy managed to jump up and reach the end of the red carpet. His weight slowly started to bring the marquee down, but he was not heavy enough to bring it completely down to the ground. Greg put a rainbow spell over the marquee to hold it steady. Andy Bear shouted to the silly chicks.

"Climb down my back as quickly as you can." The chicks being very silly chicks decided to slide down Andy Bear's back instead of carefully climbing down. They all ended up in a big heap in front of Sir Paddy and Commando Kit.

"Uhhh – ohhh," cried Chirpy in a very strange voice.

"We were only looking," said Cluck rubbing his beak, which was still sore from the maypole fall yesterday. He too sounded strange

"The big tent just floated up – we did nothing sir, honest," cried Sparks in a high pitched voice. Commando Kit pointed and said just two words.

"My office!"

43

The silly chicks did not say another word. They picked themselves up and headed off in the direction of Commando Kit's office. Danny the head snail and the other snails were now holding the ropes attached to the securing pegs.

"At the count of 3 pull the ropes together men. Andy Bear, as soon as the marquee is down, go inside and turn off the helium gas. And secure the ground pegs," ordered Commando Kit. "Sir Paddy, I will give you a full report when the marquee is secured."

"Thank you Commando Kit, I will inform Kayleigh and Florence, the nursing nightingales, to go and check the silly chicks over, then I will return to inspect the damage." Sir Paddy nodded at Commando Kit then marched off.

The marquee was now firmly secured back down on the ground. Luckily there was not too much damage, just a couple of butterfly tea lights knocked over.

"I am sorry sir. I should not have left the helium gas bottle in the marquee. I just wanted a nice surprise for Sir Paddy."

Danny lowered his head because he felt really bad this had happened.

"Danny, always run everything by me first. I can see that you wanted to do something nice, but with those silly chicks around look at the consequences." Commando Kit spoke firmly but fairly. "Did you check to make sure the helium gas was turned off?"

"Yes sir, I just don't understand – I checked it twice."

"Hmm, I have a theory. I will know more when I speak to those silly chicks."

Sir Paddy had arrived back and had a puzzled look on his face.

"Sir Paddy?" asked Commando Kit.

"There appears to be something wrong with the silly chicks voices, they are speaking in a very high voice. It is most odd. The nightingales said apart from that and Cluck's sore beak they seem to be ok."

"I think I know what happened, Sir Paddy. Danny had put a bottle of helium gas in the marquee to fill welcome balloons for Eos' visit. I suspect the silly chicks found the helium gas and inadvertently turned it on. When you inhale helium it makes your voice go very high-pitched. They probably left it on resulting in the marquee rising from the ground."

Sir Paddy, although not best pleased with the situation caused by the silly chicks, could see the funny side of it. And as no harm was done he went from a slight snigger to full blown roaring laughter. Commando Kit and Danny looked at each other then joined in.

"Those silly chicks are the bane of my life, but at least we can laugh about it," said Sir Paddy.

"Sir." Commando Kit addressed Sir Paddy. "I will question the silly chicks to confirm this, and of course I will tell them how cross everyone is. Probably better they don't know we saw the funny side of it. The whole episode caused extra work for everyone. I will put them on washing up duties for a week and confine them to the chick house."

Sir Paddy nodded then went to inspect the marquee with Commando Kit and Danny.

Everything was ready for the arrival of Eos, and as her carriage approached she could see the marquee with all the welcome balloons swaying gently. The carriage stopped and Sir Paddy followed by Commando Kit reached to open the door and greet her. Eos hugged her favourite boys making them both blush, and then they walked to the magical stream. She noticed the silly chicks all had white aprons on, and each had a little tray with a glass of sparkling water standing outside the marquee. Eos also noticed the silly chicks did not speak they just nodded. She looked at Sir Paddy who sighed and whispered.

"Will explain later Eos, let's enjoy lunch first." As Eos entered the marquee it was indeed going to be a sunset reunion.

Home Sweet Home

There is much laughter in the Sparkle Garden today. The sun is shining brightly, the birds are singing, and there is magic in the air. Today is a special day full of happiness for everyone. Eos and Sunrise had taken the girls for a trip to the canal. Lady Rosie and Lady Lily had not seen a canal boat before and were very excited. The canal boat was very long, and it was painted baby pink with glittering stars all over.

"Wow look at this Lily."

"Oh Rosie it is so pretty."

"Come on board girls, Eos and I have a surprise for you both."

Lady Rosie and Lady Lily were barking excitedly and wagging their tails. As they entered the canal boat both Rosie and Lily gasped. There were two pink sailor dresses, two pairs of pink sparkly pumps, and a pink life jacket for each girl with their name written in pink sequins, and a pink sailor hat each.

"Girls walk on further to see where you can get changed," said Sunrise. As they walked along the canal boat they found one cabin for 'Lady Rosie' and one for 'Lady Lily'. They then noticed there were also cabins for Sunrise and Eos.

"I am planning on seeing you all more often, and when I visit we will take a trip on the canal boat," cried Eos. Sunrise was smiling and there as a tear of joy in her eye. The girls were so excited they were running around chasing their tales.

"I have some news for you both." Sunrise looked at Eos and smiled. "Eos will be moving to Sir Paddy's garden." Lady Rosie and Lady Lily both gasped and started jumping up and down excitedly.

"I shall be with you for the rest of the week while my new home is being built. The stable will be extended for the golden unicorn Brian who will be sharing with the magical unicorn Greg."

"Now girls go and get changed we are going to take the canal boat out," cried Sunrise.

There was great activity in Sir Paddy's garden, and everyone was happy. The Great Oak had been chosen for Eos' new home, and a tree house was being constructed. How grand it was with a magnificent staircase at the front of the Great Oak leading to the poppy red front door. Andy Bear and Danny the head snail had been working hard with a team of snails building rooms around the branches, and how splendid it all looked. Of course the silly chicks were not allowed anywhere near the Great Oak and they were all sulking about it. They were no longer speaking in high pitched voices, which had made everyone laugh, because the helium gas had worn off.

"It's not fair – why can't we help?" complained Chirpy"

"We could do lots like ….. a… well, carry things," said Beaky

"Yer we could carry things," cried Fluffy.

"Maybe we could help with extending the stable for that other unicorn," said Cluck. All the silly chicks agreed and flapped their wings excitedly.

"That golden unicorn Brian was laughing at us when Eos came. I think the magical unicorn Greg had told him about the big tent and the funny hel – hel – that gas stuff," said Sparks.

"Well I think we should help and show him what we can do," cried Chirpy. All the silly chicks agreed and went off in the direction of the stables.

Now Brian the golden unicorn had come over to Sir Paddy's garden to help with the work to extend the stable. It was all going rather well although Brian did have some rather grand ideas.

"I think there should be pillars and a porch at the front of the stable," said Brian.

"Hmm, nice idea but it would not be right for us to have a grander entrance that Sir Paddy," replied Greg the magical unicorn.

"Yes Greg of course you are right, shall we go and have some lunch?"

Greg neighed and they trotted off to a nearby field to graze on the greenest grass in the kingdom.

"So he wants pillars, well we can do that," said Chirpy to the other silly chicks who were just in earshot of the unicorn's conversation. The silly chicks were hiding behind a bush, and when they saw the unicorns leave they rushed over to the stable.

"Look there are some lovely coloured posts over there, we could use them," cried Sparks. All the silly chicks agreed, and were in such a hurry to collect the posts they all bumped into each, other and ended up rolling all over the ground. What the silly chicks did not know was that the coloured posts were the extra supports that would be needed for the tree house. As they struggled to pick up the first post it was much heavier than they had expected.

Sir Paddy was very pleased with the tree house, and as he stood there admiring the work done by Andy Bear, Danny and the work force he enjoyed the peace and quiet. The outside building with the magnificent stair case was complete, and the poppy red front door sparkled in the sunlight. The rooms inside were still being completed, another day or so and they should be finished. Then the decoration and furniture would complete Eos's new home. As Sir Paddy turned to wander down to the stable to see how the work was coming on there he heard the cry for help. Looking up he could see something flying through the air, then he realised it was one of the silly chicks. Sir Paddy made a dash for the stable because he knew that was the direction of the silly chick's cry. As he arrived he saw the silly chick disappearing into the stable roof with all the other silly chicks clucking and rushing over to the stable. Speechless for a moment Sir Paddy just stood with his mouth open in utter disbelief. It was not long before the unicorns Greg and Brian arrived closely followed by Commando Kit and Danny the head snail.

The silly chick had been very lucky indeed. Some of the roof had been removed ready for the new larger roof to go on, and Fluffy had gone straight through the gap and landed on a nice soft pile of hay. The silly chicks all tried to rush through the stable door together, and ended up getting stuck in the doorway. Danny rushed over and gave them a big push so they all fell into the stable. Fluffy, the silly chick who had landed on the hay, was about to laugh at them when he realised they were not alone.

"Oh dear think we might be in trouble again," said Fluffy. The other silly chicks looked up and all gulped together.

"How did this happen?" Asked Commando Kit

"Well sir," said Chirpy. "We just wanted to help."

All the silly chicks were nodding. "We wanted to surprise Brian and put pillars up at the front door. They were very heavy."

"Very heavy," repeated all the silly chicks.

Chirpy continued with the explanation. "As we were trying to lift the post, Fluffy decided to take a run at it to push it upwards and thought his weight would knock it over. It went up and he lost his grip, and ended up flying through the air."

Commando Kit could see the chicks were trying to do something nice, but nevertheless it was foolhardy and Fluffy could have been hurt.

"Fluffy are you OK?" asked Commando Kit.

"Yes sir, I am fine. Are we in big trouble?"

Commando Kit turned to look at Sir Paddy, whose mouth was slightly turned in amusement. At that moment Commando Kit made his decision.

"Yes you are in trouble for 2 reasons. First you do not do any work without running it by me or Sir Paddy first. Second this could have ended with someone getting hurt. So now you will all clear up any mess, then report to the unicorns Brian and Greg for the next two days. I believe there are boxes to unpack, furniture to arrange, and any other duties they have for you."

The silly chicks were about to speak when Commando Kit silenced them with his hand.

"Together we can make this for Eos and Brian 'home sweet home'."

Razzle Dazzle Party

The silly chicks were not happy, because Brian the golden unicorn complained about everything.

"The chair is not in the right place, or, the towels are not folded the right way," mimicked Chirpy. All the other silly chicks were clucking in agreement.

"He said I slopped the water and made a mess in the yard," cried Sparks.

"Did you hear him when he trotted off this morning?" asked Beaky

"Yer I heard him." Said Fluffy and in a silly voice he repeated what Brian had said.

"Make sure the straw on my bed is nice and even."

All the silly chicks laughed at Fluffy's impersonation of Brian.

"Why can't he sort his own bed out?" cried Cluck.

"Greg the magical unicorn always makes his OWN bed," said Beaky.

"Hmm," said Chirpy, and all the silly chicks looked at him and then gathered round to see what Chirpy was thinking.

Lady Rosie and Lady Lily were spending another wonderful day on the canal boat, and would soon be approaching the magical lock to take them onto the higher level canal. It looked like a Ferris wheel with a large compartment on the lower level, and another larger compartment on the higher level. The girls were very excited and a little afraid about sailing into the compartment to be lifted to the higher level.

"It is only for a short time, and you will see a wonderful view, girls," soothed Eos. "It is another route to take us back home, and then we will be getting ready for the party this evening. Lady Rosie and Lady Lily were holding paws and not entirely sure they wanted to go to the higher level canal. The girls skipped off to play talking about the party later.

"I think the girls are a little nervous Eos." Eos put her hand on Sunrise's arm. "It is a new and exciting experience for them Sunrise, but we will make sure our girls are safe."

They were now ready to enter the compartment, and when the canal boat was securely in place the lock-gates shut tight. Eos, Sunrise and the girls were all standing on deck watching with excitement, and a little anticipation as the canal boat started to rise from the lower level. They had reached the higher level, and were waiting for the lock gates to open when they heard a loud bang, and Sunrise noticed the compartment seemed to be filling with more water around their boat. Eos had noticed too, and it was not long before Lady Rosie and Lady Lily realised that something was not right. Eos spoke to the girls to try and keep them calm.

"Girls the lock has worked perfectly."

She put her hand up because the girls were about to start asking questions. "It seems something has bumped into the gates outside, now don't worry help is on its way."

Sir Paddy was chatting with Commando Kit.

"I am looking forward to the party this evening, and the men have done a splendid job getting everything ready."

"Indeed Sir Paddy they have all worked hard, including the silly chicks who have been working tidying the stable for Brian,"

"I am looking forward to my good friend Sir Alfie arriving."

Sir Alfie was another fellow Westie Knight. They had both been to Westie Knight training together and had a very strong bond.

"Yes sir, I believe he will be arriving within the hour, and Brian will be collecting Eos, Sunrise, Lady Rosie and Lady Lily later on."

Danny the head snail came rushing into Sir Paddy's office, and both Commando Kit and Sir Paddy turned to him in surprise.

"Sirrrr." Danny was out of breath but managed to continue. "The lock gate is stuck."

Sir Paddy was puzzled and looked at Commando Kit. Commando Kit nodded his head in a knowing gesture to Sir Paddy then turned to Danny and spoke in a calm voice.

"Danny is the canal boat with Eos, Sunrise and the girls at the magical lock?"

"Yes sir, the lock compartment got to the next level but something is blocking the door, and the compartment is filling with more water."

"We must leave immediately," cried Sir Paddy.

Now Paddy had a phobia about canal boats, and it went back to when he was a young pup. He was so small back then, and the first time he ever saw a canal boat it seemed so big. What really un-nerved him was the loud horn that went off when it went passed him. It gave him such a fright he jumped into the air, and all the ducks had laughed at him. Since then he had never been near any canal boats nor had he ever spoken to anyone about it.

"Sir Paddy!" cried Danny, "The Kingfisher Michael saw it all. Eos sent him a message to get help, and he is outside sir." Sir Paddy forgot about his phobia because he was so concerned about his most favourite girls in the world, and Eos and Sunrise. They all headed for the 4 x 4

53

which had special pulling gear attached, and set off for the magical lock.

The silly chicks saw the 4 x 4 pull away with Commando Kit driving.

"Where are they all going?" asked Sparks.

"Never mind about them, Brian will be back, so soon let's get our little surprise ready for him," said Chirpy, and all the silly chicks agreed. They planned to fill his bed with soft wet mud, and then cover it in straw. This would make it very comfortable, but it would also turn a white unicorn a shade of brown. The chicks worked very hard to complete this task, but then decided perhaps it was a step too far. In a mad rush all the chicks were trying to empty Brian's bed of the soft wet mud when disaster happened. The weight of the mud was too heavy for the bed and the bottom collapsed. All the mud ran out from under the bed and covered all the silly chicks. They were covered all over, and all you could see in the shadow of the stable was 5 pairs of eyes belonging to the silly chicks.

Sir Paddy jumped out of the 4 x 4 and was confronted by a panic stricken Mrs Duck. It appeared her nest had somehow come loose, and had ended up crashing into the magical lock with her four ducklings quacking in fear. Before Commando Kit had a chance to assess the situation Sir Paddy had put the life-ring on, and attached it to the special pulling gear on the 4 x 4 before jumping into the canal. He made his way over to the nest and ducklings and pulled them safely to the bank where Mrs Duck was waiting. Commando Kit ordered Danny to operate the pulling gear, and once Sir Paddy and the ducklings were safely out of the water Commando Kit inserted the lock key and opened the gates. The water rushed our causing the canal boat to drop down quickly, but everyone was safe and well. Sir Paddy was a hero with all the ducks, and there was a large crowd of them now. One of the elder ducks gave apologies for the time they laughed at Sir Paddy all those years ago. Sir Paddy put his paw to his mouth to let him know it was not general knowledge. The unicorns Brian and Greg had arrived - they had been informed by Danny's men. They were now going to escort Eos, Sunrise and the girls back home, and bring them to the party later.

The silly chicks were exhausted, because the mud had been really difficult to clean up. Then they had to repair the bed, and then find lots of clean straw. They were still covered in mud themselves when they ran into Lancelot, Sir Paddy's steed, who was waiting for the arrival of Alfonso Sir Alfie's steed.

"What have you silly chicks been up to now?" enquired Lancelot.

"We fell over." replied Cluck.

"After cleaning up," said Sparks

"We have done a good job." cried Chirpy.

"Well Brian does always praise you silly chicks, and you do look as if you have been working hard. You better go and get cleaned up for the party tonight."

The silly chicks did not say another word, and now they all felt bad because Brian had been sticking up for them all along,

What a wonderful evening it was and everyone was happy. Sir Paddy and Sir Alfie were dancing with Lady Rosie and Lady Lily to the music 'In the cool of evening everything is looking kind of groovy' with Andy Williams singing. Commando Kit, Eos and Sunrise were drinking champagne with the unicorns Brian and Greg. Danny and all the other snails were having a lovely game of snap and eating crumpets. Lancelot and Alfonso were having their favourite drink a glass of Pimm's. Andy Bear, Sammy the beautiful butterfly, Kayleigh and Florence the nursing nightingales, and Michael the Kingfisher were playing crazy golf. And as for the silly chicks, they were fast asleep in the chick house, just too tired to go to the Razzle Dazzle Party.

Campfire Sing Song

'Ta Dah,' said Eos to herself. She had now been living in her magnificent tree house in The Great Oak for a while now, and so far the silly chicks had managed to stay out of trouble. Now Eos suspected that their attendance to the Squire School had something to do with the beautiful teacher owl Amy, who had the longest eye lashes Eos had ever seen. She had a lovely soothing voice, and those big brown eyes had a special magic about them. Eos smiled to herself because she had also noticed that Commando Kit was very fond of Amy, and he liked to check in person daily that all was well at the Squire School. But of course the silly chicks being the silly chicks were already talking about throwing an end of term surprise party for Amy, but this could only lead to one thing, which is trouble.

Sir Paddy had been working on a project to install a lift onto the outside of the Great Oak tree house, because this would make shopping or installing furniture much easier. The lift had been fitted with a red velvet carpet, and a lovely mirror on each wall with twinkling spot lights. It was shiny silver on the outside with automatic sliding doors. How pleased Sir Paddy was when he looked at the finished lift. Danny, the head snail, his team of men and Andy Bear had done a splendid job. Commando Kit had now joined Sir Paddy.

"The electrics have been tested for the lift Sir Paddy, and the men have used the lift a few times with no problems."

"Excellent Commando Kit, as soon as Eos arrives back with Sunrise, Lady Rosie and Lady Lily please escort them over to the tree house. I would like to surprise them by travelling down in the new lift, and when the doors open I will have flowers for them all."

"No problem sir, I will escort the ladies over when they arrive at tea time. I will send Sammy the butterfly over to let you know when we are approaching the tree house. The camp fire has been built to keep everyone warm this evening while the sausages are being cooked."

"It is wonderful to have the girls stay for a week, and the new lift will make it so much easier to take the luggage to the tree house."

Sir Paddy smiled and then turned to Commando Kit. "It is end of term for the Squire School tomorrow, and as the silly chicks have behaved so well I think we should have a little party. Amy the teacher owl has done a wonderful job keeping them out of trouble. What do you think about a disco in the barn?"

"That can be arranged Sir Paddy, and I know Danny the head snail has some karaoke equipment which could be fun. Amy would enjoy an end of term party."

Commando Kit blushed a little, and Sir Paddy pretended he did not notice.

Meanwhile the silly chicks had already borrowed Danny's karaoke equipment. They just wanted to see how it works.

"Let's test the karaoke out in the chick house first," cried Chirpy. "And if it works ok we can then ask Danny if we can borrow it for the end of term party for lovely Amy."

Chirpy went all starry eyed, and all the other silly chicks went 'aaahhhhhh' together.

"Yes, yes," cried Fluffy, as he grabbed the plug and rushed over to the extension socket to plug it in.

Lady Rosie and Lady Lily were very excited. They were on their way with Sunrise and Eos in the Rainbow Crown Carriage pulled by the magical unicorn Greg. They would be staying for the week at Eos' tree and house, and they were looking forward to seeing their beloved Sir Paddy. They had so many lovely friends that lived in Sir Paddy's garden, and they were looking forward to chatting with the nursing nightingales Kayleigh and Florence, Sammy the beautiful butterfly, and meeting Amy the teacher owl. The carriage came to a stop, and Commando Kit immediately went to open the door for the girls.

"Welcome ladies I will take you straight to Sir Paddy."

Lady Rosie and Lady Lily giggled as they took Commando Kit's hand to leave the carriage. Just before they got to the tree house Sammy had signalled to Sir Paddy to travel down in the lift. Lady Rosie and Lady Lily were amazed when they saw the lift, and they could see the light on the control panel by the door flashing showing the lift was on its way down.

"Noooooooo," cried Danny as he saw Fluffy put the plug into the extension socket, but it was too late. There was a bang then everything went black. All the lights had gone out, and it seemed the power was lost everywhere.

"Uh-oh, I think we are in trouble again," cried Fluffy in the darkness. They could also hear the cross voice of Commando Kit in the distance, which made them all very nervous.

"You idiots, plugging in my karaoke equipment into an extension socket you have over-loaded the system," said Danny crossly. Commando Kit had spoken to him earlier about using his karaoke equipment for the end of term party. Danny had gone to get it from his room but it had gone. He saw the trail of feathers and followed them to the chick house, but was just too late to stop the silly chicks from using the extension socket.

Sir Paddy gulped when the lift came to a stop and all the lights went out. He stood very still for a moment, and then remembered he had a small torch in his pocket. Lady Rosie and Lady Lily were clinging onto Eos and Sunrise, and both girls were shaking.

"It's alright girls just the electricity gone off for a moment. Commando Kit will sort it out," soothed Sunrise. Commando Kit immediately gave the order for all torches to be turned on, and then for the camp fire to be lit. Andy Bear had arrived with a ladder which was placed against the side of the lift where there was an emergency escape door. Commando Kit went up the ladder and opened the door. Sir Paddy was very pleased to see him, but was not looking forward to getting on the ladder and hesitated.

"Sir Paddy we need to get you safely down then I can go and look at the fuse box."

Sir Paddy reluctantly agreed and started to descend the ladder. Danny and the silly chicks had arrived just in time to see Sir Paddy nervously climbing down the ladder. Even though they were in big trouble the silly chicks seeing Sir Paddy slowly climbing down the ladder started to point and laugh at him. When they saw Commando Kit looking at them disapprovingly they immediately stopped. Once Sir Paddy was safely down Danny turned to Commando Kit to explain.

"Sir the silly chicks had taken my karaoke equipment, because they wanted to surprise their teacher owl Amy with an end of term party. Unfortunately they didn't ask me first, and then plugged the karaoke into an extension socket which over-loaded the system."

Before Commando Kit could answer Amy, who had heard all of this, stepped forward to speak to him.

"Commando Kit the silly chicks have been a little reckless and know they have done wrong, but their hearts were in the right place. Sir Paddy is safe, and once the electricity is back on I am sure the chicks will be happy serve the drinks and sausages."

Commando Kit agreed, and when he saw Amy's big brown eyes looking at him he too was under her Magic spell. It was a lovely evening, and everyone enjoyed the campfire sing song.

Boogie Night Fun

There was great excitement in Sir Paddy's garden, and the barn
looked amazing with twinkling lights. There was a large disco ball
hanging from a beam, and the Karaoke had been set up next to the
disco. The silly chicks had been putting all the tables and chairs out
since very early in the morning on Commando Kit's orders, and were
feeling quite tired now. They had all received a big telling off from

Commando Kit last night, and each of them had to write an apology letter to Sir Paddy. This was because they had laughed at him when he was being rescued from the lift, and had to climb down a ladder.

"He did look very funny on the ladder," cried Fluffy.

"I think he was scared," said Beaky."

"Well, you silly chicks should be ashamed of yourselves. Sir Paddy is one of the bravest Knights I know," cried Mrs Duck. The silly chicks all turned to see a very cross Mrs Duck standing just behind them.

"He saved my babies when the nest broke free and crashed into the magical lock gates. Sir Paddy was so brave he jumped into the lock and got my babies out safely." Mrs Duck had her wings folded in front of her, and was tapping her foot.

"We are sorry Mrs Duck," said Chirpy. And all the chicks said together, "Yes we are sorry."

"We love Sir Paddy and have written him a sorry letter," said Sparks. Mrs Duck gave two loud quacks and left. The silly chicks all looked at each other, and then they all looked at Beaky.

"That was your fault Beaky, and now Mrs Duck is cross with us too," cried Cluck. It was not long before the silly chicks were all arguing with each other. Then one of them accidentally knocked the on switch for the Karaoke machine. And the silly chicks being silly chicks could not resist having a sing song.

Sir Paddy had taken his most favourite girls in the world Lady Rosie and Lady Lily out for morning coffee. They had gone to a rather splendid cake shop to have a delicious cup of coffee, and a piece of lemon drizzle cake. When the order arrived at their table the girls noticed there was an extra cup of coffee, and piece of cake. Before they could ask Sir Paddy any questions his good friend Sir Alfie arrived.

"Good morning beautiful ladies - Sir Paddy."

Sir Alfie gave his biggest brightest smile he could muster. Sir Paddy jumped to his feet and shook his good friend's paw. Lady Rosie and Lady Lily giggled then Sir Alfie took both their paws together and lightly kissed them. They spent a wonderful morning chatting and catching up before returning to Sir Paddy's garden.

Eos and Sunrise had been busy preparing a 'pass the parcel' filled with treats, pin the tail on the dragon, and a dragon piñatas. All the balloons were going to be inflated in the barn they just needed to take them over. No helium gas was going to be used this time, not after the trouble the silly chicks got into last time. They had accidentally turned on the helium gas, which had resulted in them all speaking in very high pitched voices for a couple of days. Eos was holding one of the balloons and smiling.

"Oh Sunrise those silly chicks with the helium gas, they did sound very funny indeed."

Sunrise laughed with her friend and told her what the nightingales had told her."

"Dear Eos the silly chicks had asked the nightingales for some medicine so they could talk properly again." Sunrise and Eos were laughing together now.

"And when the nightingales told them there was no medicine they had to wait for it to wear off, do you know what one of the silly chicks then said?"

"No, please tell me Sunrise," replied Eos through her laughter.

"He said, 'Well I thought you two were supposed to be nurses', in his high pitched voice, and then walked off in a sulk." Both Eos and Sunrise were laughing out loud.

"Well I think it is time we took everything over to the barn, and perhaps we can get the silly chicks to blow these balloons up the old fashion way using their beaks," said Eos.

Sir Paddy, Sir Alfie and the girls had arrived back at the garden, and could not believe how loud the music was. Eos and Sunrise were just behind them with their arms full of games and balloons, and they were closely followed by Commando Kit, Danny the head snail and Andy Bear. The music playing was:

'There may be trouble ahead,
But while there's music and moonlight and love and romance,
Let's face the music and dance.'

At that moment the silly chicks burst out of the barn door one by one spinning around and all falling in a big heap on the ground. Danny rushed into the barn and turned the music off. The silly chicks had their wings covering their ears, and they were not expecting to see everyone looking down at them.

"I assume you have an explanation for the loud music?" asked Commando Kit.

"It – it just started playing, and when we tried to turn it off it got louder," cried Chirpy.

"We were going to get Danny to turn it off." Sparks hesitated for a moment and then continued. "We ran to the door, but we couldn't all get out so we ended up going round in circles and got dizzy." There was a moments silence then everyone started to laugh. The silly chicks were confused, and just sat there looking at everyone. By this time there was quite a crowd, the unicorns Brian and Greg, the nursing nightingales Kayleigh and Florence, the trusted steeds Lancelot and Alfonso, Sammy the butterfly, Amy the teacher owl, Michael the kingfisher, and Mrs Duck. As soon as the laughter quietened down Commando Kit spoke to the silly chicks.

"Now on your feet chicks there is still a lot to do so everything is ready for the party this evening."

The silly chicks looked confused, but that was nothing new. Amy the owl smiled at Commando Kit, and there was much happiness in the garden.

What a wonderful party it was, and everyone enjoyed the party games Eos and Sunrise had prepared. Everyone had fun singing on the Karaoke, and the silly chicks made everyone laugh when they tried to sing 'New York, New York'. They were just singing 'If you can make it there you can make it anywhere', and kicking their legs together when they all toppled over. It was the best Boogie Night fun ever.

Paddy Stories is available as an eBook in all major online formats from Smashwords. Follow the link:

http://www.smashwords.com/books/view/324652

Also available as an eBook is **Paddy Stories - Magic of Christmas**

http://www.smashwords.com/books/view/374271

Lightning Source UK Ltd.
Milton Keynes UK
UKOW05f1902200114

224954UK00001B/54/P